My First Book of Learning

Om KIDZ
An imprint of Om Books International

First Published in 2018 by

Om Kidz | Om Books International

Corporate & Editorial Office
A-12, Sector 64, Noida 201 301
Uttar Pradesh, India
Phone: +91 120 477 4100
Email: editorial@ombooks.com
Website: www.ombooksinternational.com

Sales Office
107, Ansari Road, Darya Ganj
New Delhi 110 002, India
Phone: +91 11 4000 9000
Email: sales@ombooks.com
Website: www.ombooks.com

ISBN: 978-93-8527-370-4

Printed in India

10 9 8 7 6 5 4 3 2 1

Contents

1 One

Elephant

Practice the number **1**

2 Two
Dogs

Practice the number **2**

3 Three

Babies

Practice the number **3**

4 Four

Cats

Practice the number 4

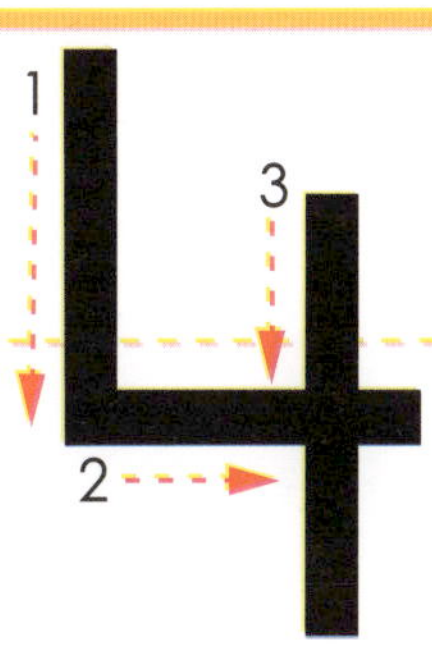

5 Five

Apples

Practice the number 5

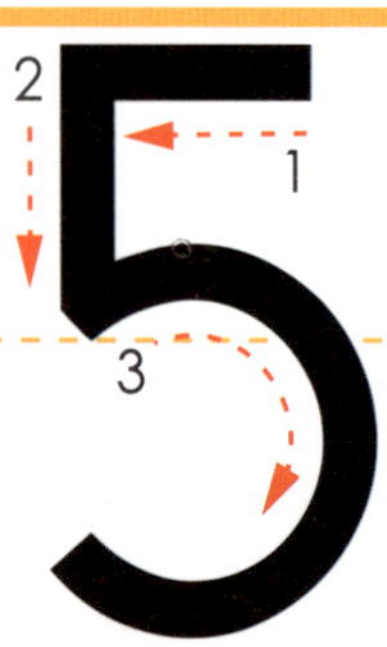

6 Six

Jugs

Practice the number **6**

7 Seven

Jokers

Practice the number 7

8 Eight

Vases

Practice the number 8

1 8

9 Nine

Eggs

Practice the number **9**

9

10 Ten Doughnuts

Practice the number 10

11 Eleven

Cupcakes

Practice the number **11**

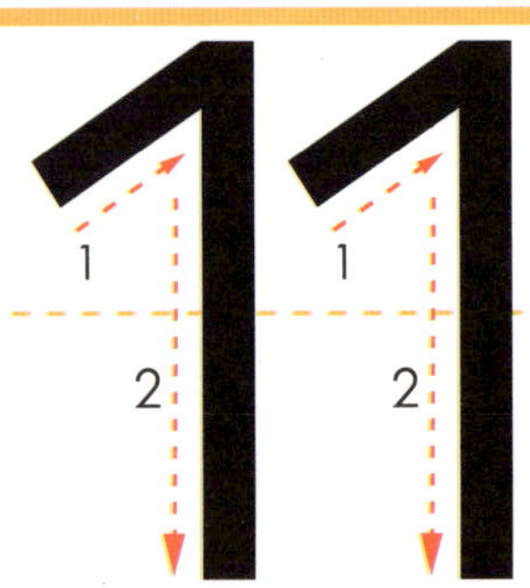

12 Twelve

Igloos

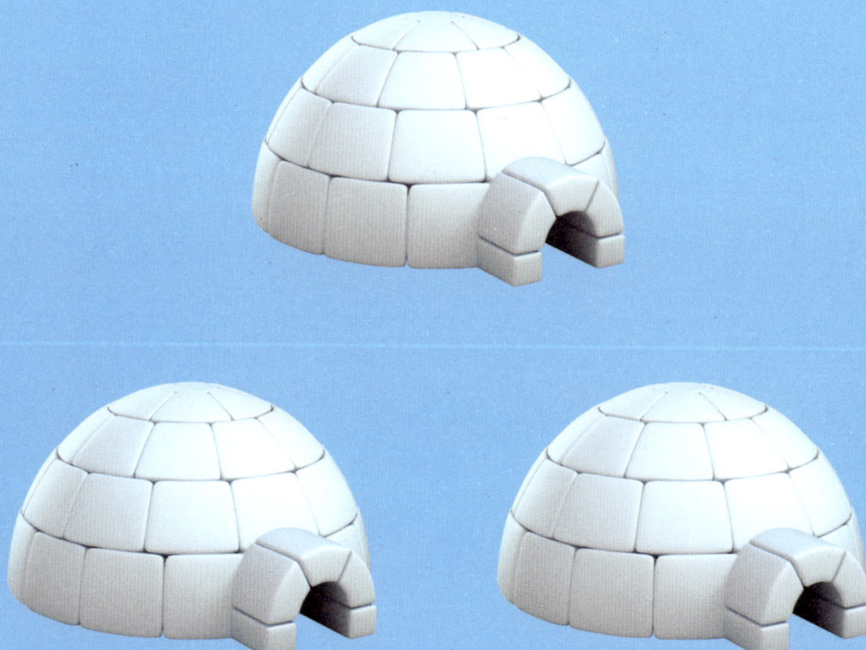

Practice the number 12

13 Thirteen

Flowers

Practice the number **13**

14 Fourteen

Pots

Practice the number **14**

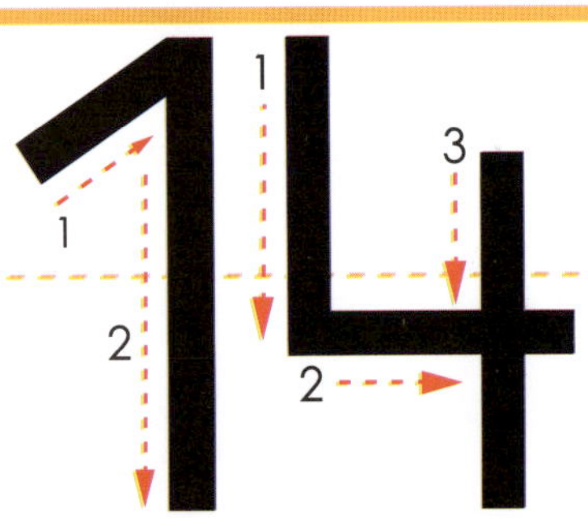

15 Fifteen

Cups

Practice the number **15**

16 Sixteen
Tomatoes

Practice the number 16

17 Seventeen

Teddy Bears

Practice the number 17

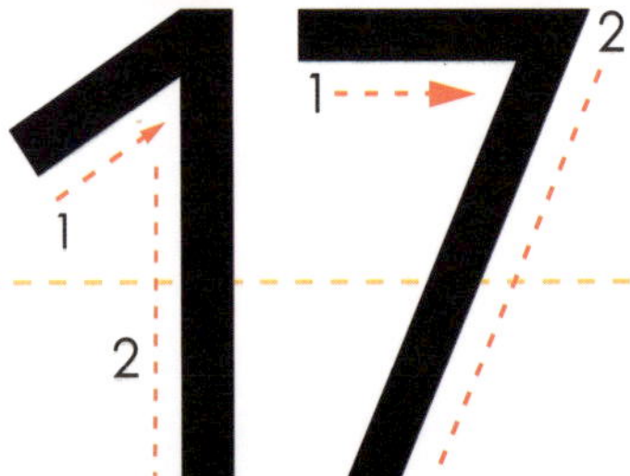

18 Eighteen

Fishes

Practice the number 18

19 Nineteen

Butterflies

Practice the number 19

20 Twenty

Hats

Practice the number 20

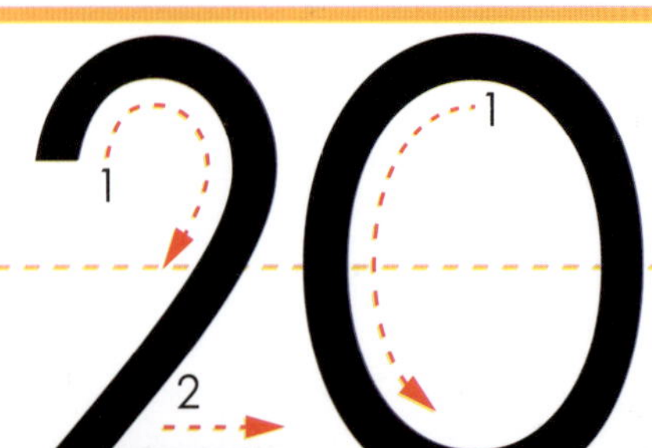

Red

Flower

Kite

Fill in the colour

Slide

Girl

Clock

Fill in the colour

Blue

Bag

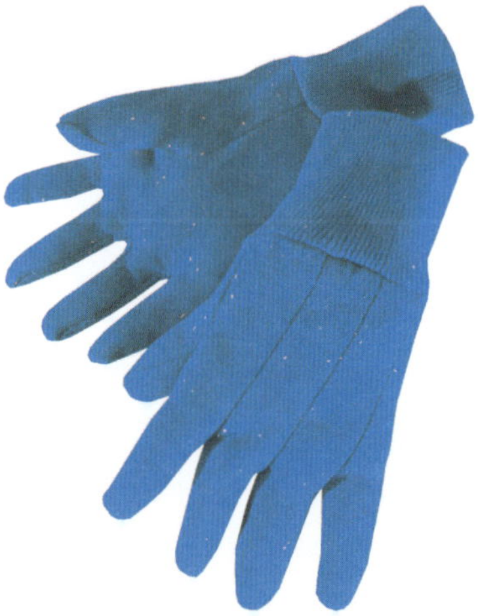

Gloves

Fill in the colour

Guitar

Jacket

Quilt

Fill in the colour

Orange

Orange

Lily

Fill in the colour

Starfish

Pumpkin

Juice

Fill in the colour

Green

Leaf

Cushion

Fill in the colour

Frog

Grapes

Watermelon

Fill in the colour

Yellow

Corn

Sunflower

Fill in the colour

Duck

Banana

Lemon

Fill in the colour

Pink

Piggy Bank

Ribbon

Fill in the colour

Candy Floss

Bow

Button

Fill in the colour

Purple

Flower

Brinjals

Fill in the colour

Gift Box

Mask

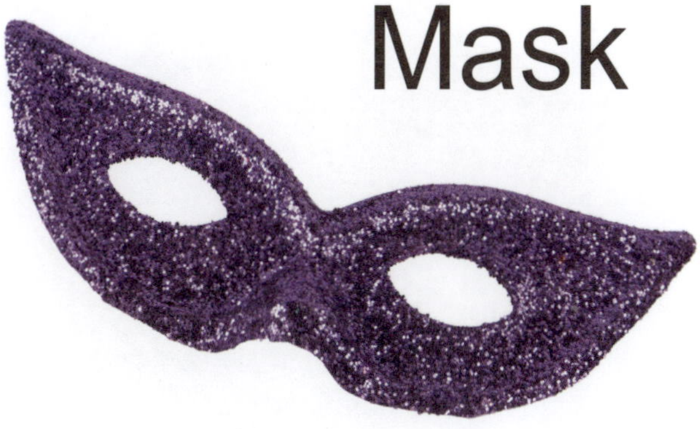

Scarf

Fill in the colour

Brown

Bread

Basket

Fill in the colour

Chocolates

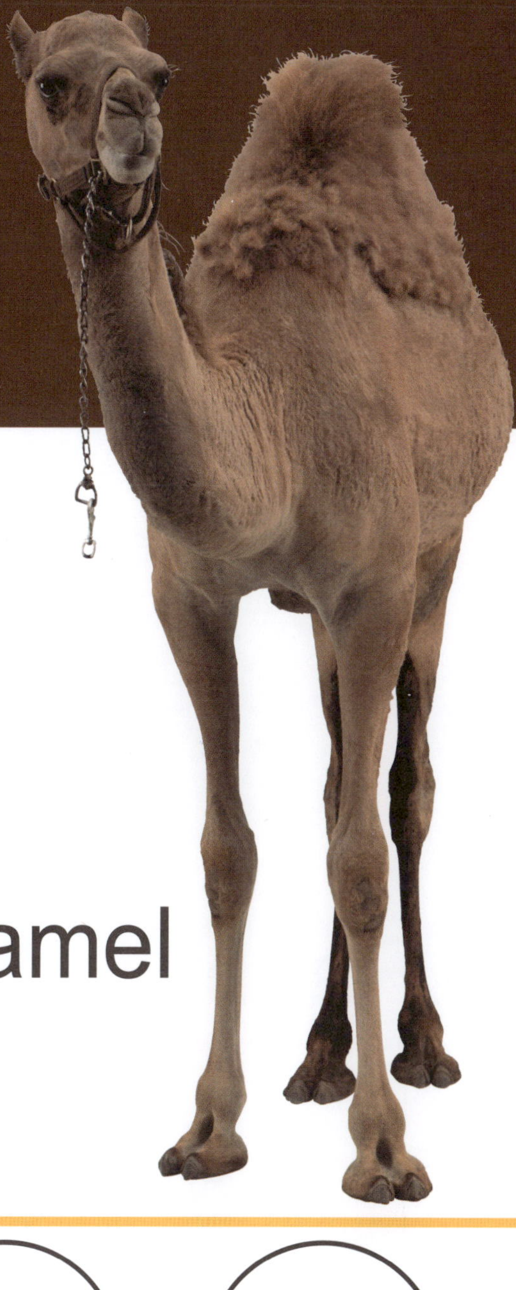

Eggs

Camel

Fill in the colour

Grey

Otter

Rabbit

Fill in the colour

Elephant

Rock

Binocular

Fill in the colour

Black

Shoes

Crow

Fill in the colour

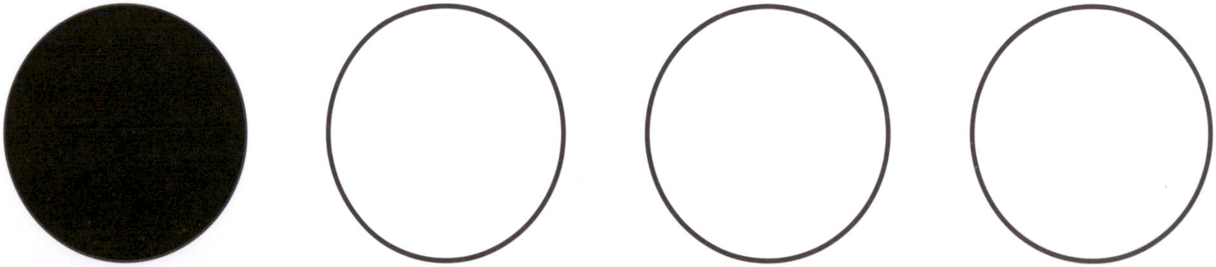

Blackboard

Umbrella

Scorpion

Fill in the colour

White

Sugar Cubes

Dove

Fill in the colour

Aeroplane

Pearls

Milk

Fill in the colour

Multi-Coloured

Bird

Xylophone

Fill in the colour

Rainbow

Puppet

Butterfly

Fill in the colour

Gold

Coins

Crown

Ring

Fill in the colour

Silver

Star

Spoon

Tea Pot

Fill in the colour

Match the following

Match the following

Fill in the matching colour

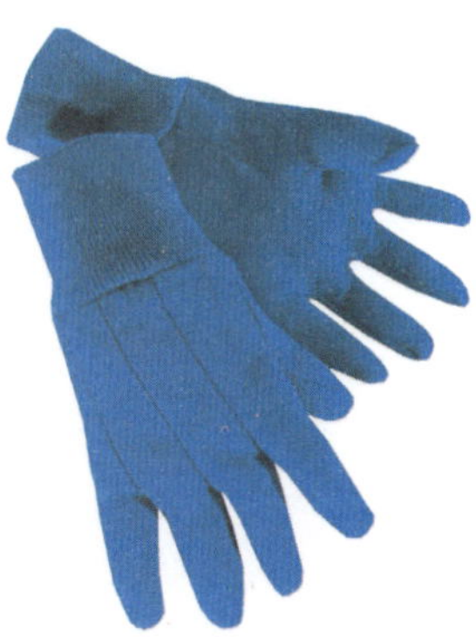

Fill in the matching colour

Circle

Ring

Flower

Practice the shape Circle

Hat

Clock

Dart Board

Square

Chess Board

Tiles

Practice the shape Square

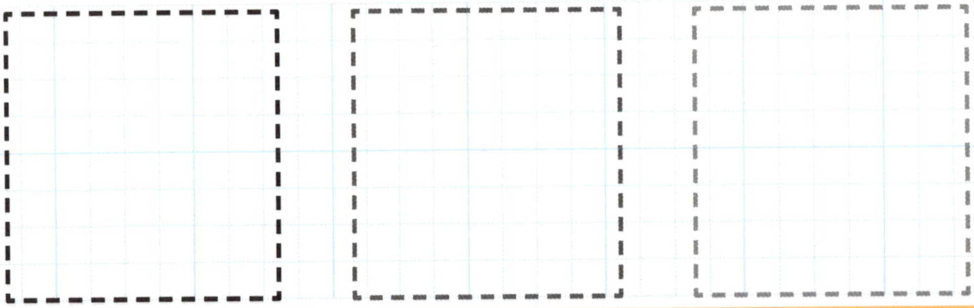

Cushion

Frame

Crackers

Triangle

Hanger

Christmas Tree

Practice the shape Triangle

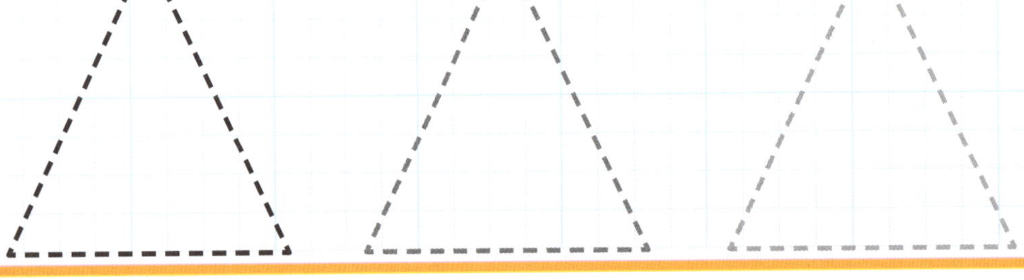

Sandwich

Sign Board

Pyramid

Rectangle

Shoe Box

Books

Practice the shape Rectangle

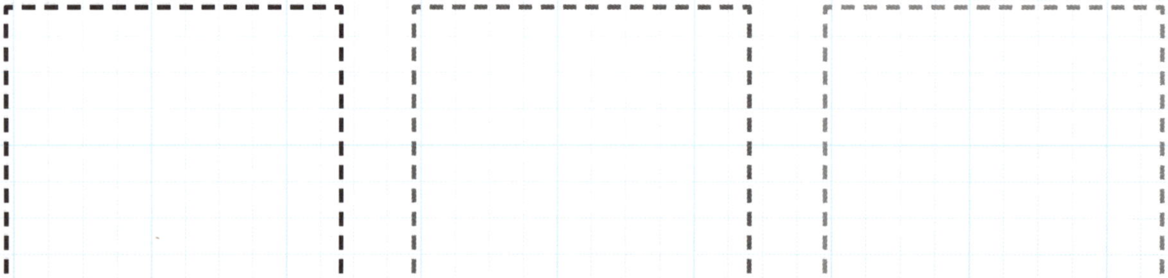

Bags

Envelope

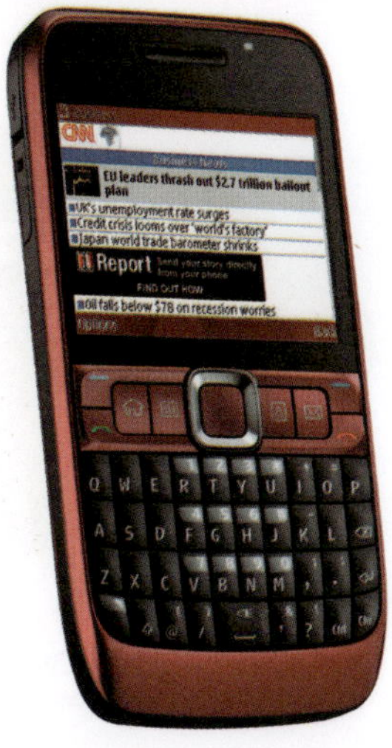

Mobile

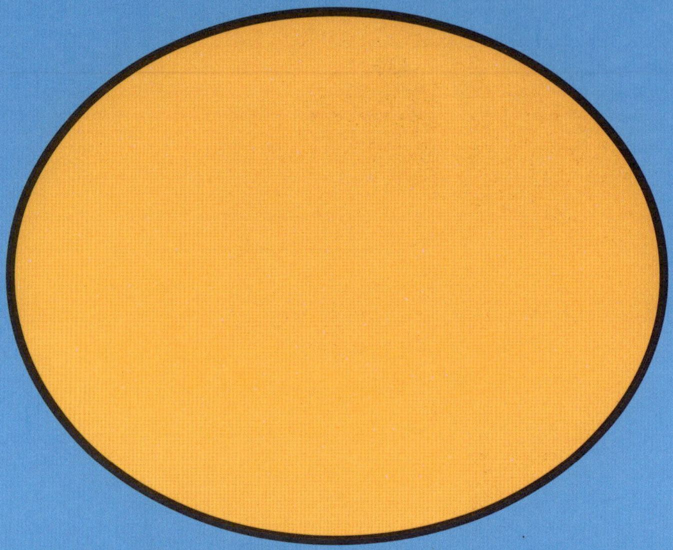

Oval

Tray

Rugby Ball

Practice the shape Oval

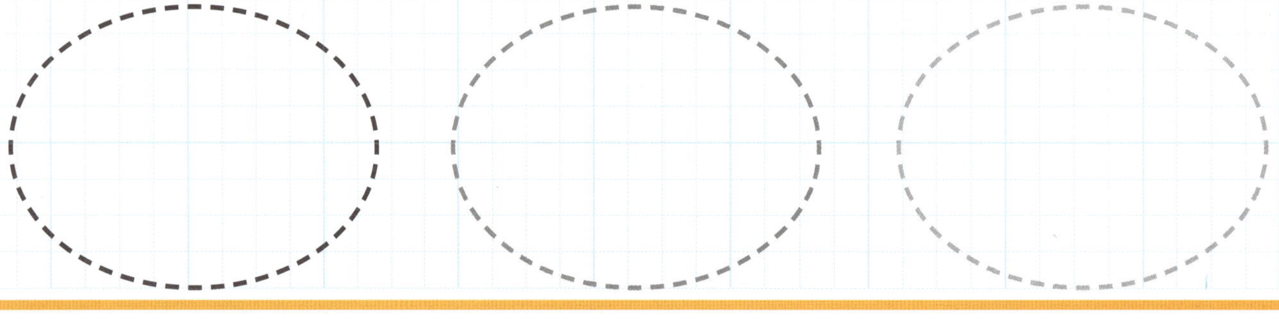

Eggs

Mask

Mirror

Heart

Gift Box

Chocolates

Practice the shape Heart

Candies

Strawberries

Cake

Star

Key Ring

Christmas Star

Practice the shape Star

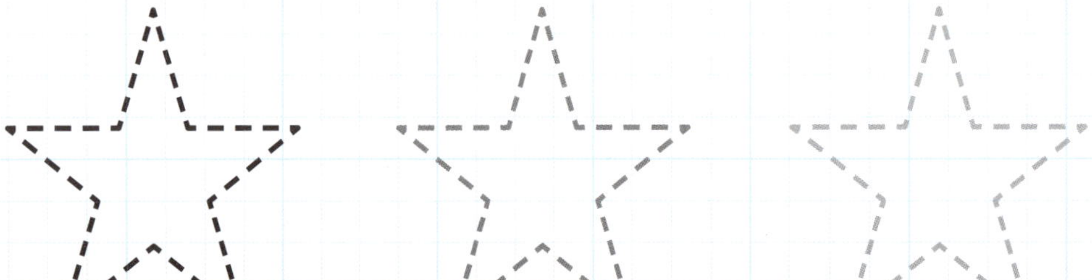

Starfish

Star Fruit

Medal

Cylinder

Mug

Soup Can

Practice the shape Cylinder

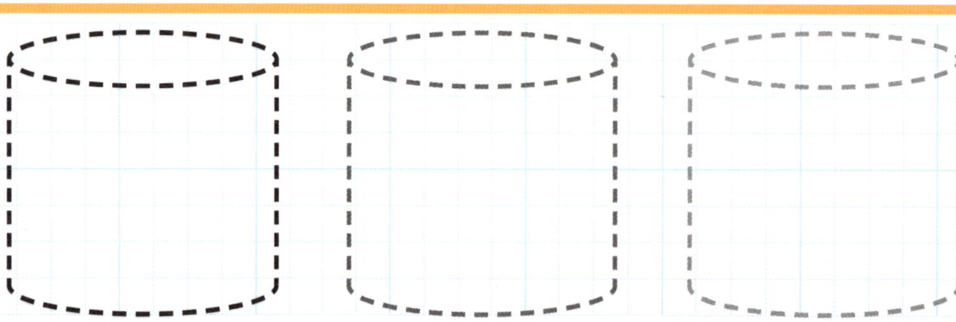

Soft Drink Can

Glass

Spool

Cube

Dice

Box

Practice the shape Cube

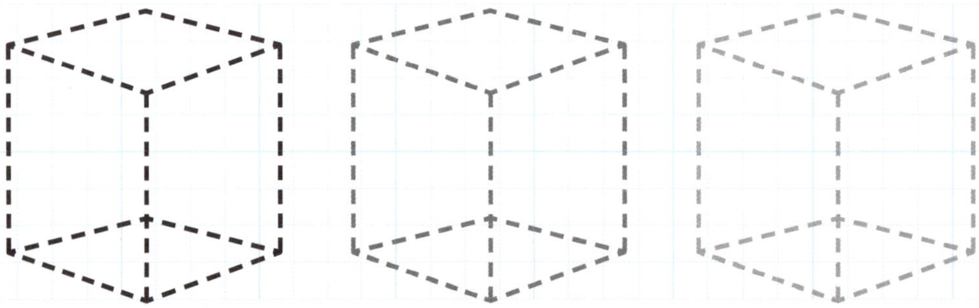

Rubik's Cube

Ice Cubes

Sugar Cubes

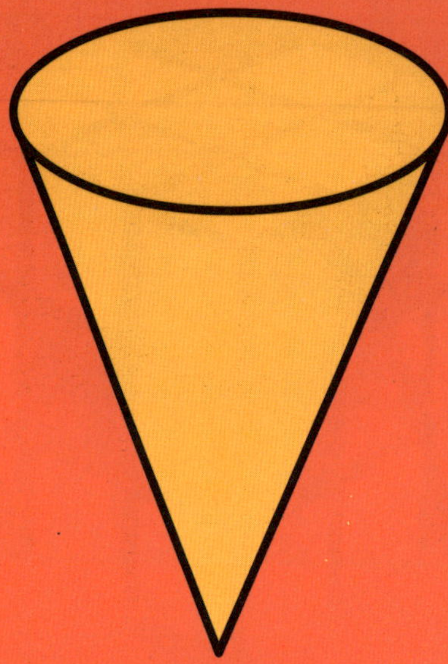

Cone

Ice Cream Cone

Traffic Cone

Practice the shape Cone

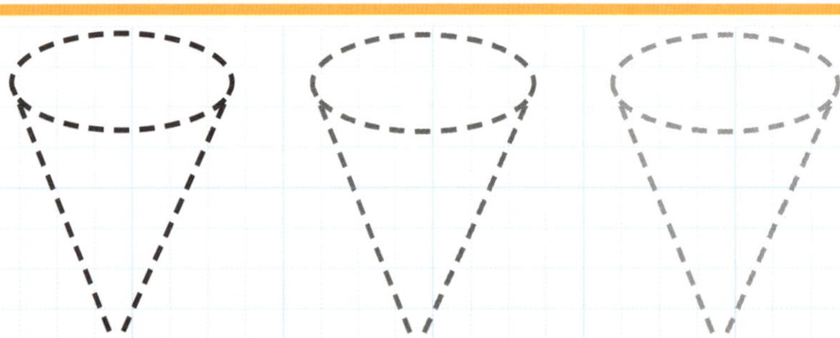

Megaphone

Funnel

Cap

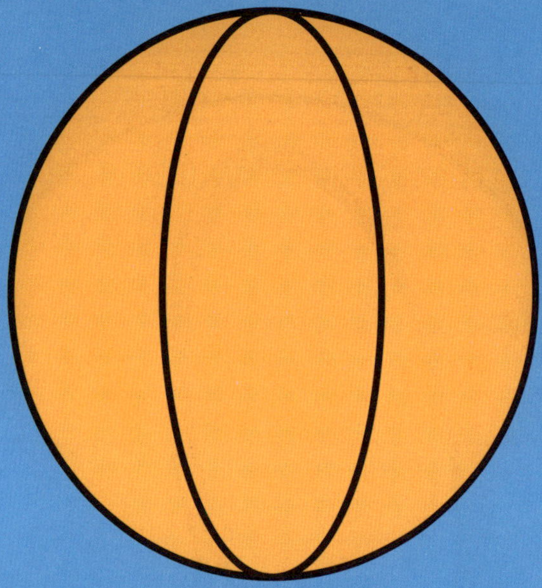

Sphere

Globe

Ball

Practice the shape Sphere

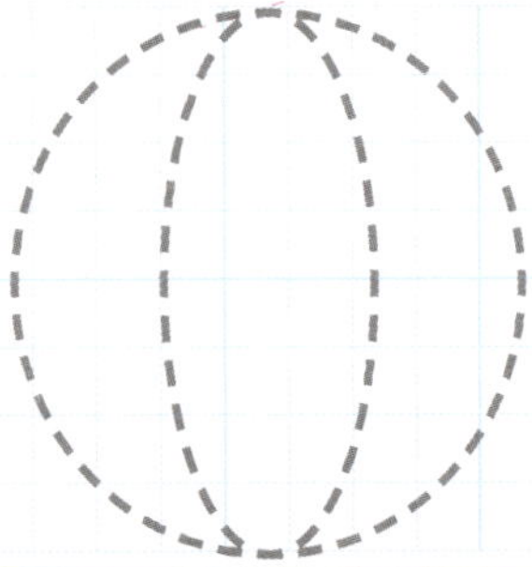

Semi-circle

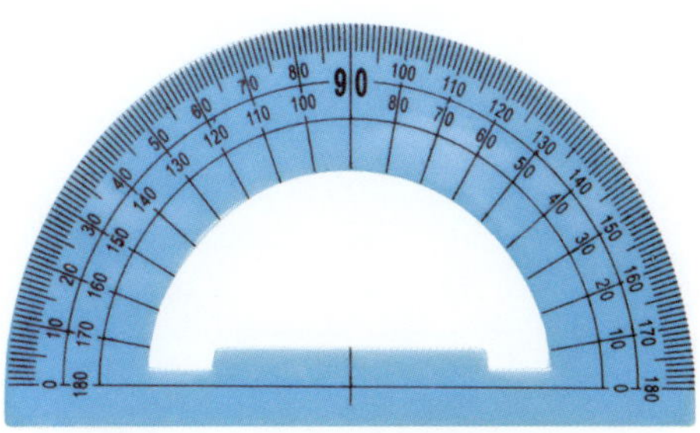

Protractor

Hand Fan

Practice the shape Semi-circle

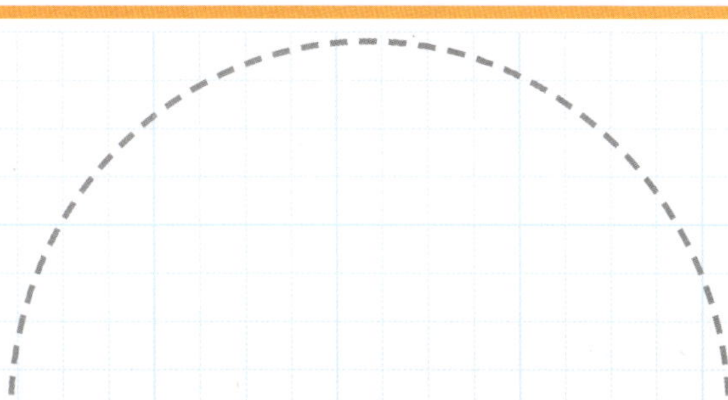

Hexagon

Plate

Jewellery Box

Practice the shape Hexagon

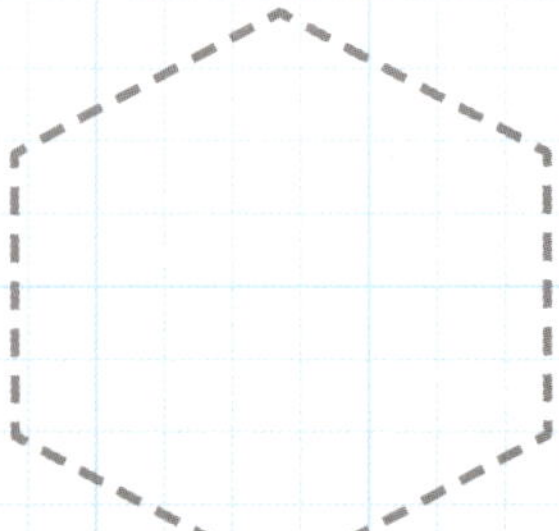

Rhombus

Clock

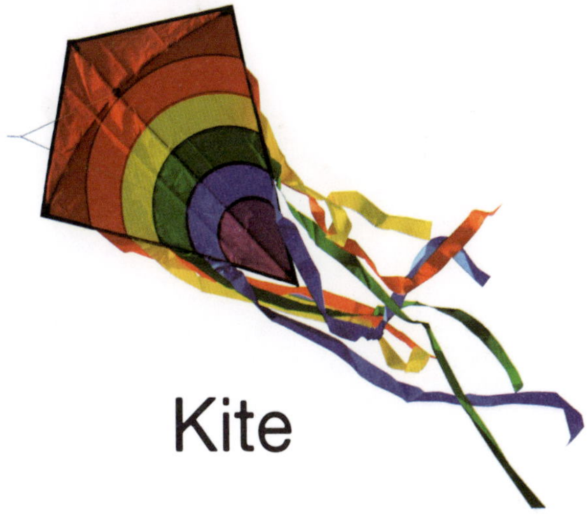

Kite

Practice the shape Rhombus

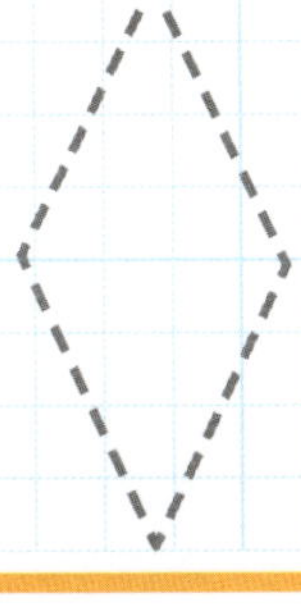

Zigzag

Brackets

Bracelet

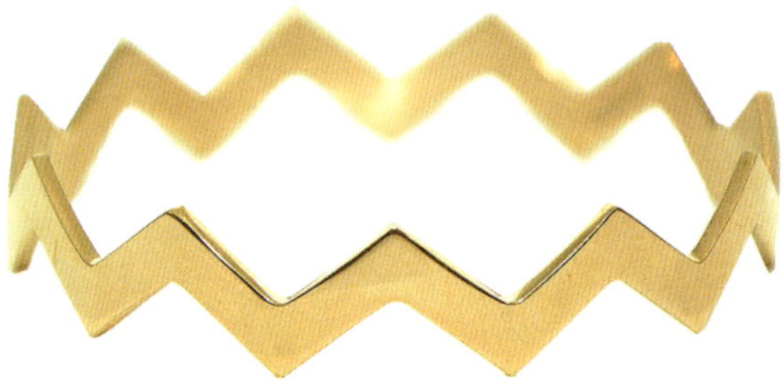

Practice the shape Zigzag

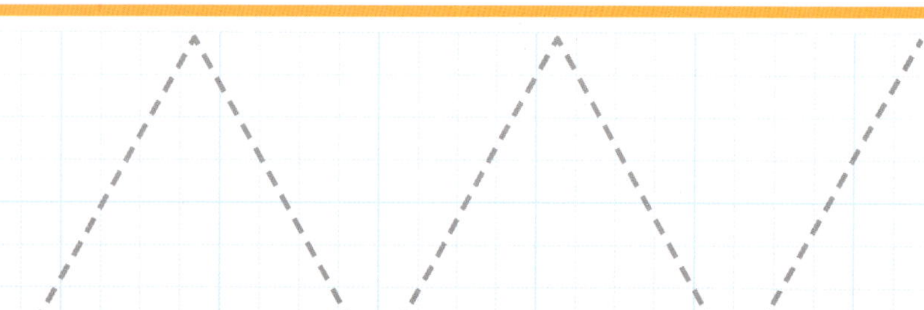

Spiral

Spring

Cord

Practice the shape Spiral

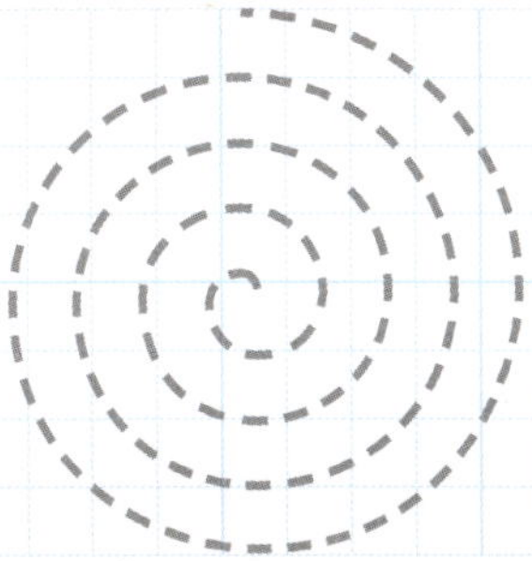

Practice Page

Practice Page

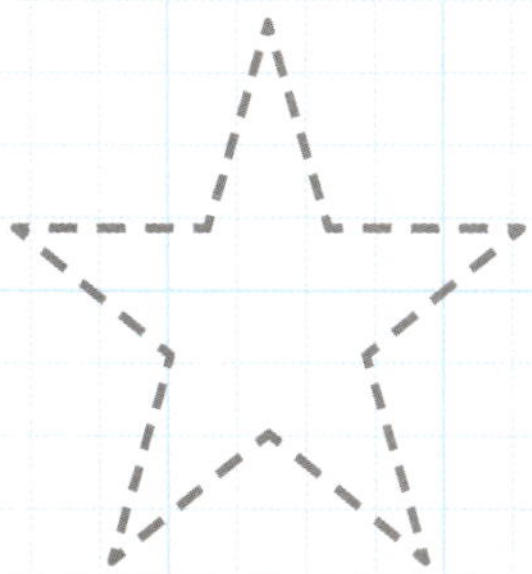

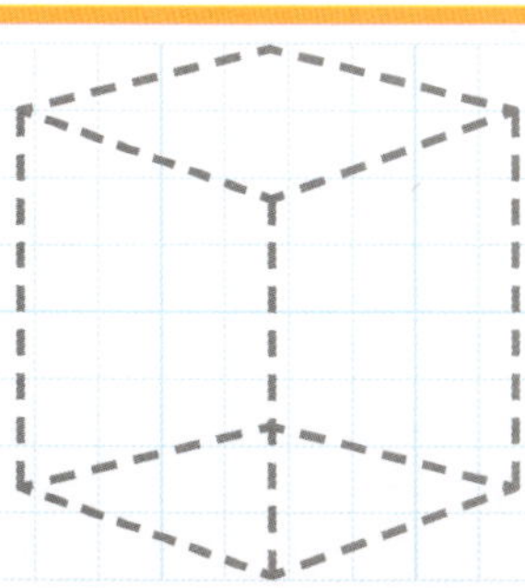

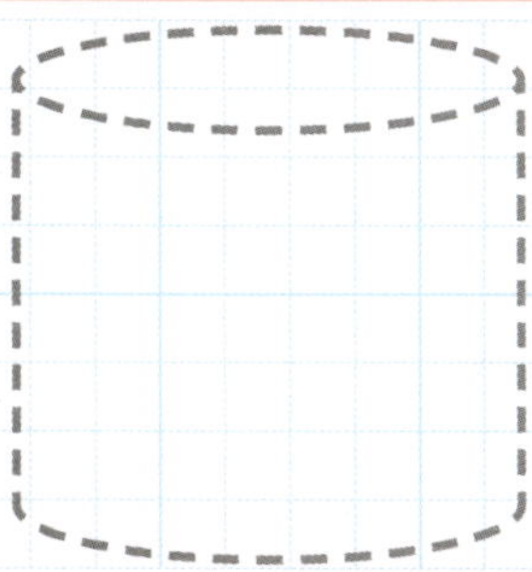

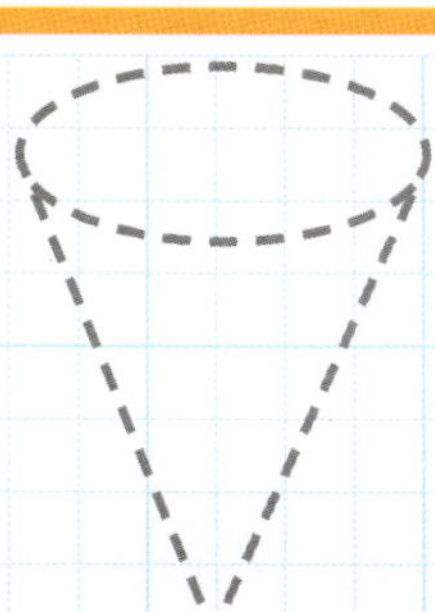

Practice Page

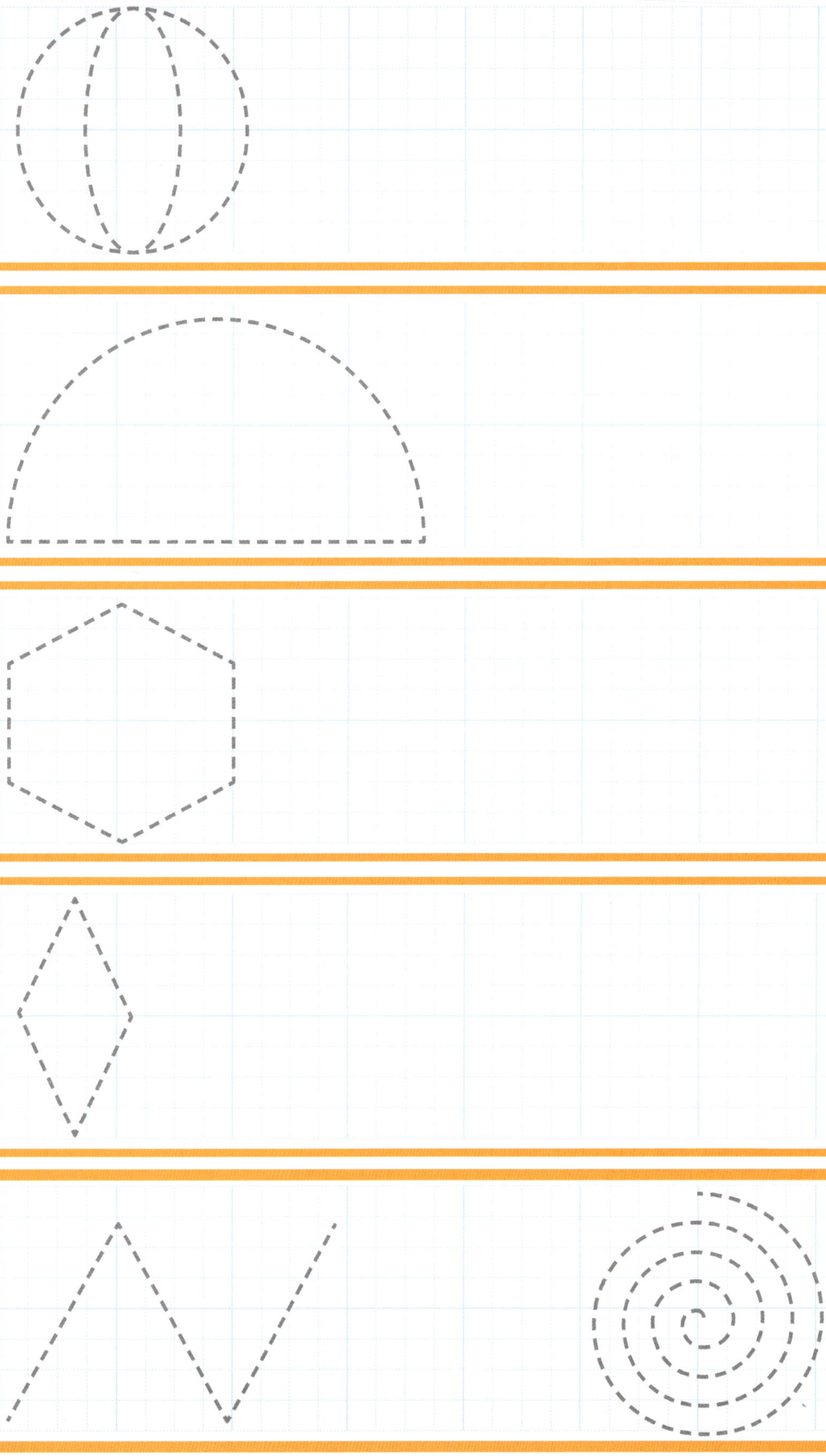

Match the following

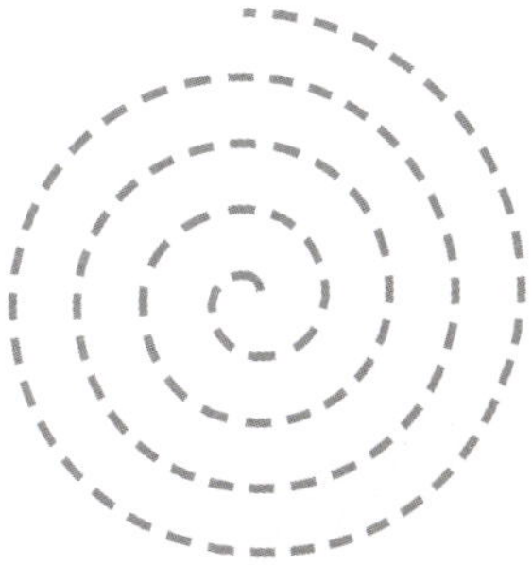

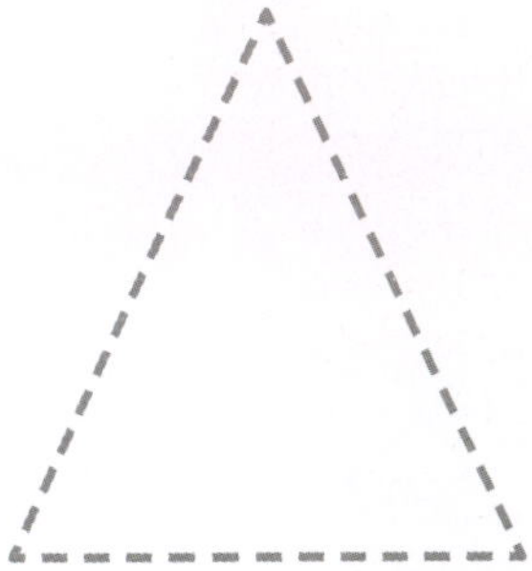

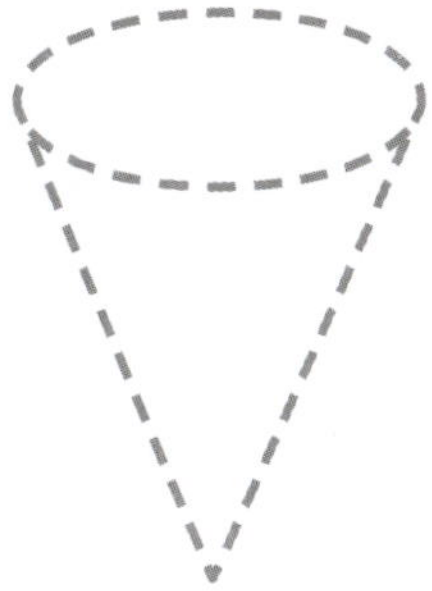

A

Apple

Practice the alphabet A

1 2

A

3

B

Baby

Practice the alphabet **B**

C

Candy

Practice the alphabet **C**

C

D

Dog

Practice the alphabet **D**

D

E

Elephant

Practice the alphabet E

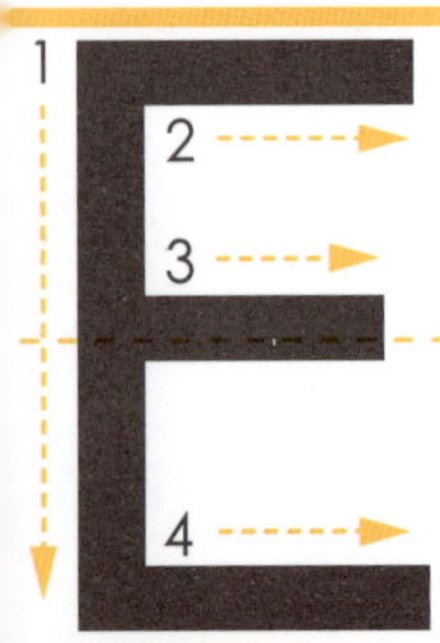

F

Frog

Practice the alphabet F

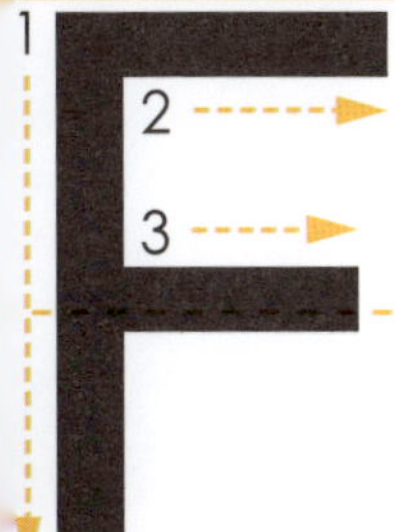

G

Giraffe

Practice the alphabet G

G

H

Hippo

Practice the alphabet H

1 H 3
2

I

Ice Cream

Practice the alphabet I

1

J

Jug

Practice the alphabet **J**

1 J

K

Kite

Practice the alphabet K

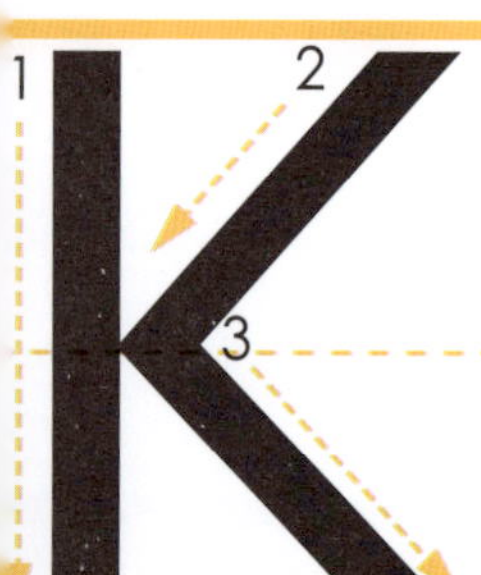

L

Lion

Practice the alphabet L

1

L

2

M

Milk

Practice the alphabet M

1 2 3 4

M

Nuts

N

Practice the alphabet **N**

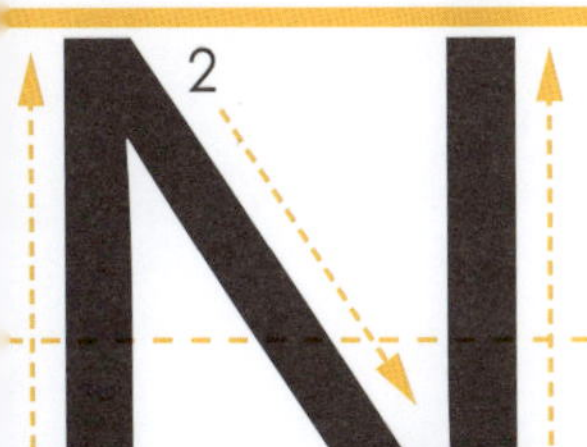

O

Orange

Practice the alphabet O

O

P

Pot

Practice the alphabet **P**

Q

Quilt

Practice the alphabet **Q**

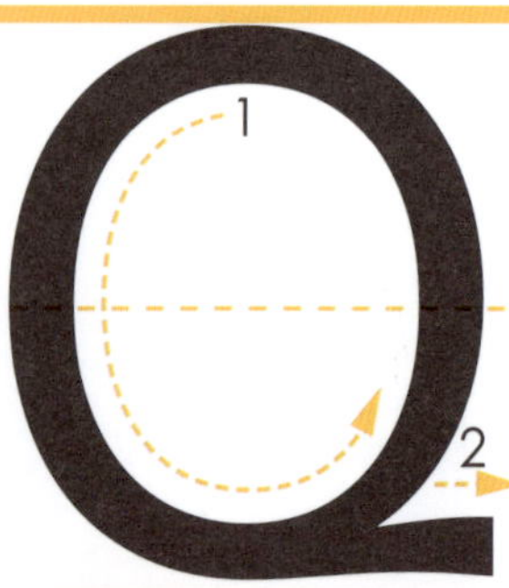

R

Rabbit

Practice the alphabet R

R

S

Sugar Cubes

Practice the alphabet S

S

T

Teddy Bear

Practice the alphabet T

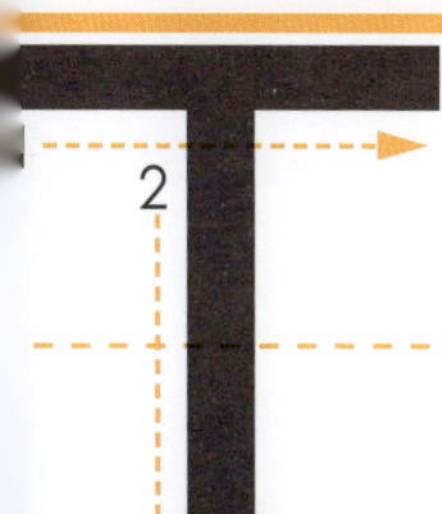

U

Umbrella

Practice the alphabet U

U

V

Violin

Practice the alphabet **V**

V

W

Wheel

Practice the alphabet W

1 2 3 4

W

Xylophone

X

Practice the alphabet X

X

Y

Yo-yo

Practice the alphabet Y

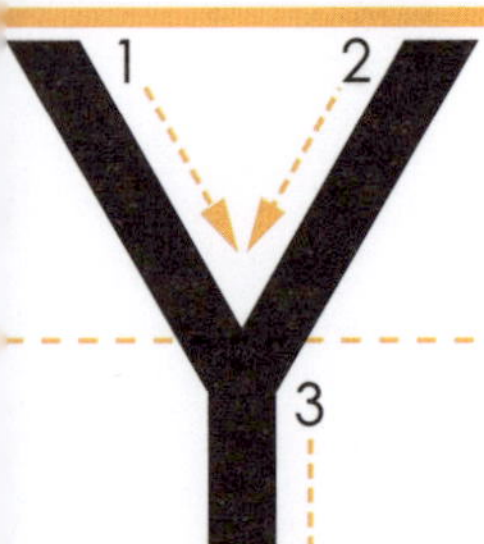

Z

Zebra

Practice the alphabet Z

Z

1 2 3

Practice the alphabet

A

B

C

D

E

F

G

H

I

J

K

L

M

Practice the alphabet

N

O

P

Q

R

S

T

U

V

W

X

Y

Z

Match the following

Frog

Ice Cream

Umbrella

Dog

Teddy Bear

Match the following

Hippo

Lion

Orange

Jug

Wheel

Pets

Dog

Tick the correct answer ✓

A dog is a colour / pet.

Cat

Fish

Parrot

Rabbit

Tick the correct answer ✓

A fish is a pet / furniture.

Wild Animals

Tiger

Tick the correct answer ✓

A bear is a bird / wild animal.

Lion

Elephant

Bear

Leopard

Tick the correct answer ✓

A lion is a wild animal / flower.

Birds

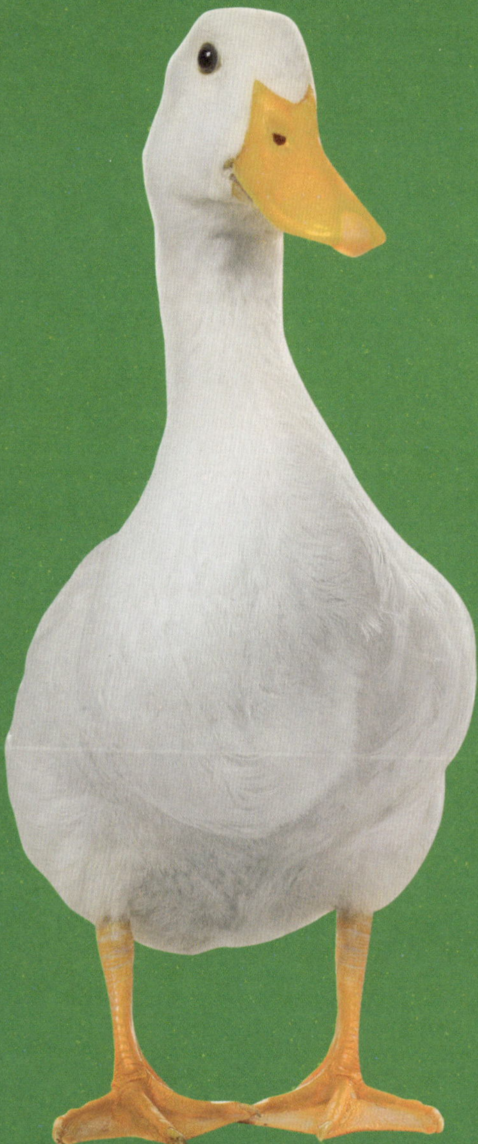

Duck

Tick the correct answer ✓

An owl is a vehicle / bird.

Dove

Owl

Ostrich

Sparrow

Tick the correct answer ✓

A sparrow is a bird / fruit.

Fruits

Mango

Tick the correct answer ✓

A mango is a pet / fruit.

Apple

Grapes

Bananas

Strawberry

Tick the correct answer ✓

An apple is a fruit / clothing.

Vegetables

Onion

Tick the correct answer ✓

An onion is a furniture / vegetable.

Potato

Carrot

Okra

Tomato

Tick the correct answer ✓

A tomato is a vegetable / bird.

Games

Dart Board

Tick the correct answer ✓

Cricket is a game / fruit.

Cricket

Football

Blocks

Carrom

Tick the correct answer ✓

Football is a wild animal / game.

Flowers

Rose

Tick the correct answer ✓

A rose is a flower / pet.

Lotus

Daisy

Sunflower

Lily

Tick the correct answer ✓

A lily is a bird / flower.

Colours

Red

Tick the correct answer ✓

Red is a colour / flower.

Blue

Black

Green

Yellow

Tick the correct answer ✓

Blue is a vehicle / colour.

Desserts

Cake

Tick the correct answer ✓

A cupcake is a vegetable / dessert.

Chocolates

Ice Cream

Cupcake

Custard

Tick the correct answer ✓

An ice cream is a dessert / furniture.

Baby Animals

Puppy

Tick the correct answer ✓

A cub is a flower / baby animal.

Kitten

Cub

Chick

Calf

Tick the correct answer ✓

A chick is a baby animal / vehicle.

Crockery

Bowl

Tick the correct answer ✓

A plate is crockery / a vehicle.

Cup

Teapot

Jar

Plate

Tick the correct answer ✓

A bowl is a wild animal / crockery.

Snacks

Popcorn

Tick the correct answer ✓

Noodles are a snack / colour.

Noodles

Biscuits

Sandwich

Chips

Tick the correct answer ✓

Chips are a bird / snack.

Furniture

Sofa

Tick the correct answer ✓

A chair is a furniture / dessert.

Chair

Table

Bed

Stool

Tick the correct answer ✓

A table is a bird / furniture.

Clothing

Jacket

Tick the correct answer ✓

A frock is a clothing / vegetable.

Frock

Shirt

Trousers

Skirt

Tick the correct answer ✓

A skirt is a fruit / clothing.

Vehicles

Bus

Tick the correct answer ✓

A truck is a clothing / vehicle.

Scooter

Van

Truck

Cycle

Tick the correct answer ✓

A van is a vehicle / pet.

Slow

Fast

Tortoise

Rabbit

Tick the correct word ✓

Opposite of Slow is Fast/Small

Slow	Fast

Tricycle

Bike

Tick the correct word ✓

Opposite of Fast is Slow/Big

Big Small

Ship

Boat

Tick the correct word ✓

Opposite of Big is Small/Slow

Big	Small

Tennis Ball

Football

Tick the correct word ✓

Opposite of Small is Big/Fast

Solid

Liquid

Water

Ice

Tick the correct word ✓

Opposite of Solid is Cold/Liquid

Solid

Liquid

Cheese

Milk

Tick the correct word ✓

Opposite of Liquid is Hot/Solid

Hot

Cold

Ice Cream

Noodles

Tick the correct word ✓

Opposite of Hot is Cold/Liquid

Hot

Cold

Soup

Milkshake

Tick the correct word ✓

Opposite of Cold is Hot/Solid

Heavy   Light

Bicycle

Bus

Tick the correct word ✓

Opposite of Heavy is Fat/Light

Heavy Light

Stone

Feather

Tick the correct word ✓

Opposite of Light is Heavy/Thin

Fat	Thin

Fat Man

Thin Man

Tick the correct word ✓

Opposite of Fat is Thin/Light

Fat

Thin

Fat Dog

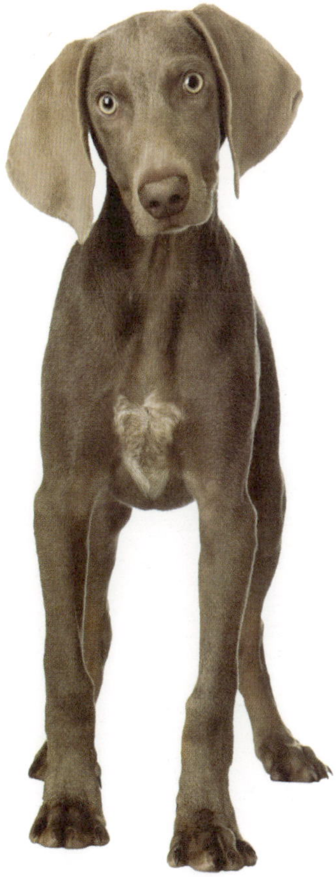

Thin Dog

Tick the correct word ✓

Opposite of Thin is Heavy/Fat

Open	Shut

Shut Cupboard

Open Cupboard

Tick the correct word ✓

Opposite of Open is Shut/Many

Open

Shut

Shut Window

Open Window

Tick the correct word ✓

Opposite of Shut is Few/Open

Few Many

Many Balloons

Few Balloons

Tick the correct word ✓

Opposite of Few is Open/Many

Few | Many

Few Candies

Many Candies

Tick the correct word ✓

Opposite of Many is Few/Shut

Old

New

Old Sofa

New Sofa

Tick the correct word ✓

Opposite of Old is New/White

Old

New

Old Gloves

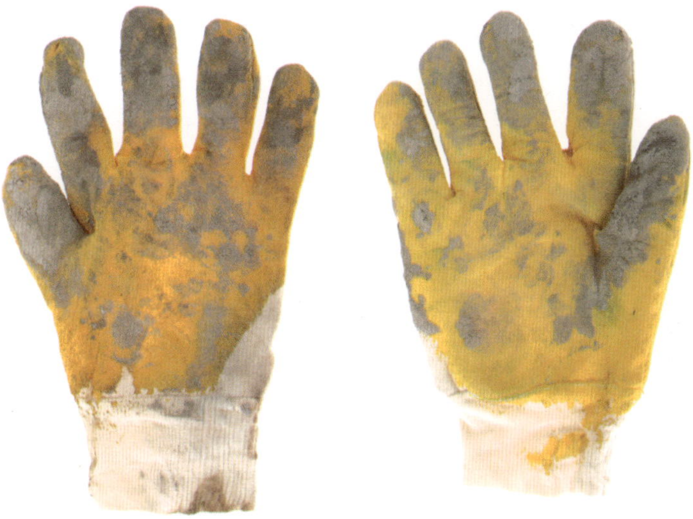

New Gloves

Tick the correct word ✓

Opposite of New is Black/Old

Black	White

Black Cat

White Cat

Tick the correct word ✓

Opposite of Black is Old/White

Black White

Black Shoes

White Shoes

Tick the correct word ✓

Opposite of White is Black/New

Long

Short

Long Skirt

Short Skirt

Tick the correct word ✓

Opposite of Long is Sweet/Short

Sweet

Sour

Mango

Lemon

Tick the correct word ✓

Opposite of Sweet is Sour/Long

Happy Sad

Happy Baby

Sad Baby

Tick the correct word ✓

Opposite of Happy is Sad/High

Low	High

Bungalow

Sky Scrapers

Tick the correct word ✓

Opposite of Low is High/Sad

Standing Sitting

Standing Giraffe

Sitting Giraffe

Tick the correct word ✓

Opposite of Standing is Wide/Sitting

Narrow | Wide

Narrow Tree

Wide Tree

Tick the correct word ✓

Opposite of Narrow is Sitting/Wide

Front Back

Front

Back

Tick the correct word ✓

Opposite of Front is Day/Back

Day

Night

Tick the correct word ✓

Opposite of Day is Front/Night

Boy Girl

Boy

Girl

Tick the correct word ✓

Opposite of Boy is Up/Girl

Up Down

Down

Up

Tick the correct word ✓

Opposite of Up is Down/Boy

Spinach

Lettuce

Mustard Greens

Fill in the blank

Sp_nach is very good for health.

Cabbage

Swiss
Chard

Fill in the blank

Cab_age is a crunchy vegetable.

Onion

Garlic

Spring Onion

Fill in the blank

G_rlic can fight common cold.

Shallot

Turnip

Fill in the blank

Tur_ips are rich in Vitamin C.

Carrot

Beetroot

Radish

Fill in the blank

Ca_rots grow underground.

Ginger

Horseradish

Fill in the blank

Gi_ger has soft, thin skin.

Potato

Sweet Potato

Chinese Yam

Fill in the blank

_otato was first grown in South America.

Fill in the blank

Lo_us Stem is not a flower.

Asparagus

Celery

Fennel

Fill in the blank

Fenn_l seeds are used as a cooking ingredient.

Kohlrabi

Rhubarb

Fill in the blank

Rhu_arb grows all year round.

Beans

Okra

Drumsticks

Fill in the blank

O_ra is also called lady's finger.

Peas

Fava Beans

Fill in the blank

P_as are contained within a pod.

Artichoke

Green Chilli

Broccoli

Fill in the blank

_reen chilli is very spicy.

Cauliflower

Bell Pepper

Fill in the blank

C_uliflower is not a flower.

Bitter Gourd

Bottle Gourd

Yellow Zucchini

Fill in the blank

B_tter gourd grows on creeper plants.

Snake Gourd

Kabocha

Fill in the blank

Ka_ocha is also called Japanese pumpkin.

Baby Corn

Bok Choy

Butternut Squash

Fill in the blank

Baby _orn is small in size.

Chayotes

Pineapple
Guava

Fill in the blank

Pineapple _uava is not a fruit.

Turnip Greens

Watercress

Collard Greens

Fill in the blank

Tu_nip Greens are rich in calcium.

Parsley

Lemongrass

Fill in the blank

_emongrass is a tropical plant.

Snow Peas

Stem Lettuce

Arugula

Fill in the blank

Snow _eas are flat and green.

Broccoli
Rabe

Vine Spinach

Fill in the blank

_ine Spinach is also called Malabar Spinach.

Basil

Mint

Chives

Fill in the blank

Mi_t is an aromatic herb.

Coriander

Rosemary

Fill in the blank

Coria_der is also called Cilantro.

Tomato

Cherry Tomato

Cucumber

Fill in the blank

C_cumbers are used to make salads.

Eggplant

Pumpkin

Fill in the blank

E_gplant is also called Aubergine.

Brussels
Sprout

Lima Beans

Fenugreek
Leaves

Fill in the blank

Brusse_s Sprouts have rough skin.

Jicama

Acorn Squash

Fill in the blank

Acorn Squ_sh looks like a Pumpkin.

Match the following

Basil • • 

Broccoli • • 

Pineapple Guava • • 

Pumpkin • • 

Beetroot • • 

Match the following

Sweet Potato	
Bitter Gourd	
Green Peas	
Onion	
Turnip	

Apricot

Pear

Grapefruit

Fill in the blank

G_apefruits grow on trees.

Apple

Water Chestnut

Fill in the blank

_ater chestnuts grow underwater.

Mango

Passion Fruit

Banana

Fill in the blank

Mang_es are sweet and juicy.

Coconut

Pineapple

Fill in the blank

A C_conut has a hard shell.

Muskmelon

Honeydew
Melon

Canary
Melon

Fill in the blank

Ca_ary melons are oval in shape.

Watermelon

Horned Melon

Fill in the blank

Wat_rmelons grow in the summer.

Lime

Lemon

Citron

Fill in the blank

Lem_ns are used to make lemonade.

Tangerine

Orange

Fill in the blank

_angerines are sweet and tangy.

Blackberry

Gooseberry

Blueberry

Fill in the blank

Bl_eberries are used to make jam and jelly.

Cranberry

Raspberry

Fill in the blank

Cr_nberries grow on shrubs and vines.

Damson Plum

Dates

Miracle Berry

Fill in the blank

Dams_n plums are not as sweet as plums.

Cloudberry

Cashew Apple

Fill in the blank

C_shew apples are red in colour.

Peach

Lychee

Ugli Fruit

Fill in the blank

U_li fruits have a rough skin.

Nectarine

Java Apple

Fill in the blank

Ja_a apples have waxy skin.

Pomegranate

Guava

Rose Hip

Fill in the blank

Po_egranates are red in colour.

Hedge Apple

Papaya

Fill in the blank

_apayas are also called pawpaws.

Kiwi

Avocado

Quince

Fill in the blank

A_ocados have green skin.

Fig

Plum

Fill in the blank

P_ums taste sweet and tangy.

Cheese Fruit

Loquat

Ground Cherry

Fill in the blank

Ch_ese fruit is also called Noni.

Wood Apple

Breadfruit

Fill in the blank

Bre_dfruit looks like Jackfruit.

Grapes

Cherry

Strawberry

Fill in the blank

G_apes are black, red and green in colour.

Currant

Jujube

Fill in the blank

Ju_ubes are also called Chinese dates.

Rambutan

Dragon Fruit

Star Fruit

Fill in the blank

_ragon fruits are common in Asia.

Mangosteen

Kumquat

Fill in the blank

Ku_quats are citrus fruits.

Red Mulberry

Persimmon

Clementine

Fill in the blank

Clementi_es look like oranges.

Sapote

Custard Apple

Fill in the blank

Custa_d apples have rough skin.

Pomelo

Goji Berry

Tamarillo

Fill in the blank

Pome_o looks like a Grapefruit.

Salak

Butternut Squash

Fill in the blank

Sa_ak is also called Snake Fruit.

Match the following

Cherry • 

Guava • 

Dragon Fruit • 

Plum • 

Cashew Apple • 

Match the following

Lychee •	• 
Pear •	• 
Passion Fruit •	• 
Lemon •	• 
Peach •	• 

Bicycle

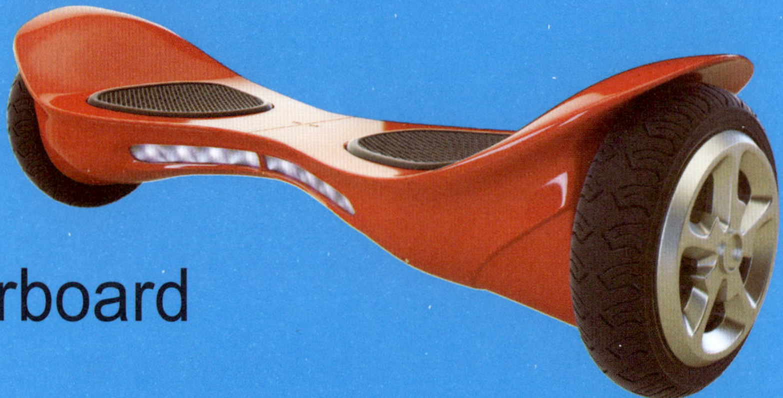

Hoverboard

Tick (✓) the correct answer

A bicycle has four wheels / two wheels.

Motorcycle

Scooter

Tick (✓) the correct answer

A motorcycle has an engine / umbrella.

Cycle Rickshaw

Tricycle

Tick (✓) the correct answer

A cycle rickshaw has three wheels / hands.

Auto Rickshaw

Quad Bike

Tick (✓) the correct answer

A quad bike has thick tyres / tiny tyres.

Car

Train

Tick (✓) the correct answer

A car runs on fuel / juice.

Bus

Truck

Tick (✓) the correct answer

A truck is driven by a driver / bird.

Ferry Boat

Bus

Tick (✓) the correct answer

Ferry Boats carry people / air.

Metro

Monorail

Tick (✓) the correct answer

Monorails are a form of public / private transport.

Ship

Sail Boat

Tick (✓) the correct answer

A ship is headed by a captain / driver.

Tick (✓) the correct answer

A kayak floats on a river / farm.

Airplane

Helicopter

Tick (✓) the correct answer

An Airplane flies in the water / air.

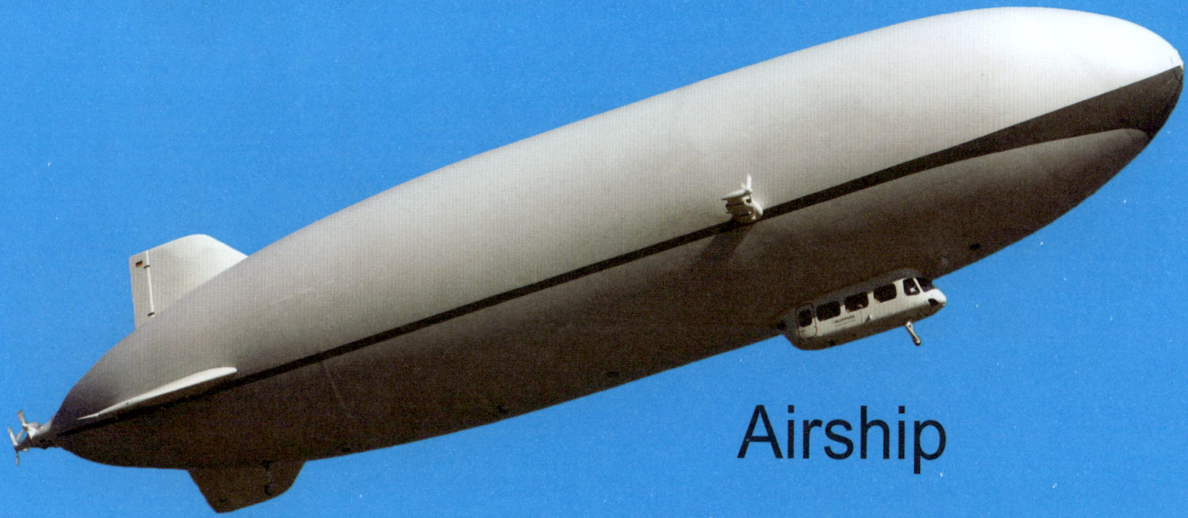

Tick (✓) the correct answer

A Glider is a type of plane / toy.

Rocket

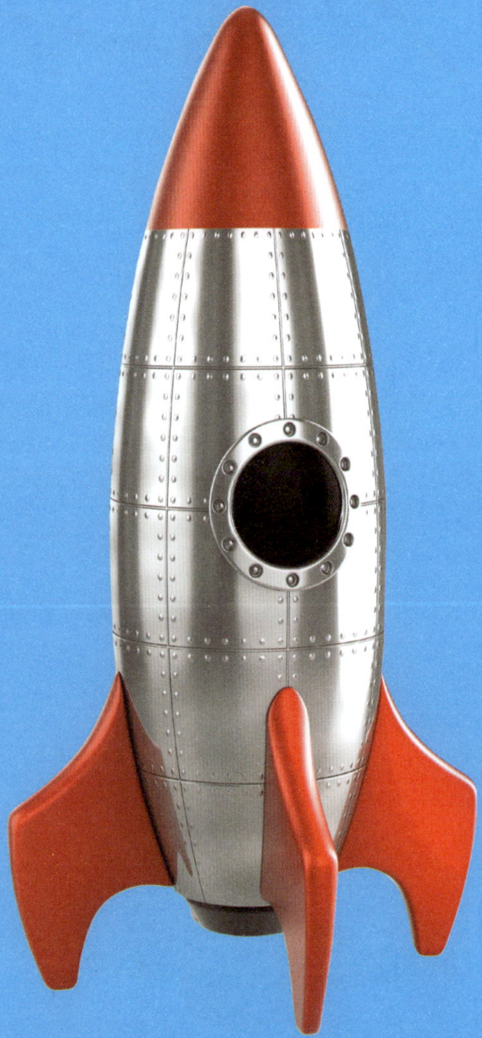

Jump Jet

Tick (✓) the correct answer

Rockets are sent to space / school.

Spaceship

Space Capsule

Tick (✓) the correct answer

Space Capsules carry information / leaves.

Cable Car

Gondola Lift

Tick (✓) the correct answer

Cable Cars run on cables / cabins.

Tram Car

Rail Wagon

Tick (✓) the correct answer

A tram Car runs on water / tracks.

Fire Engine

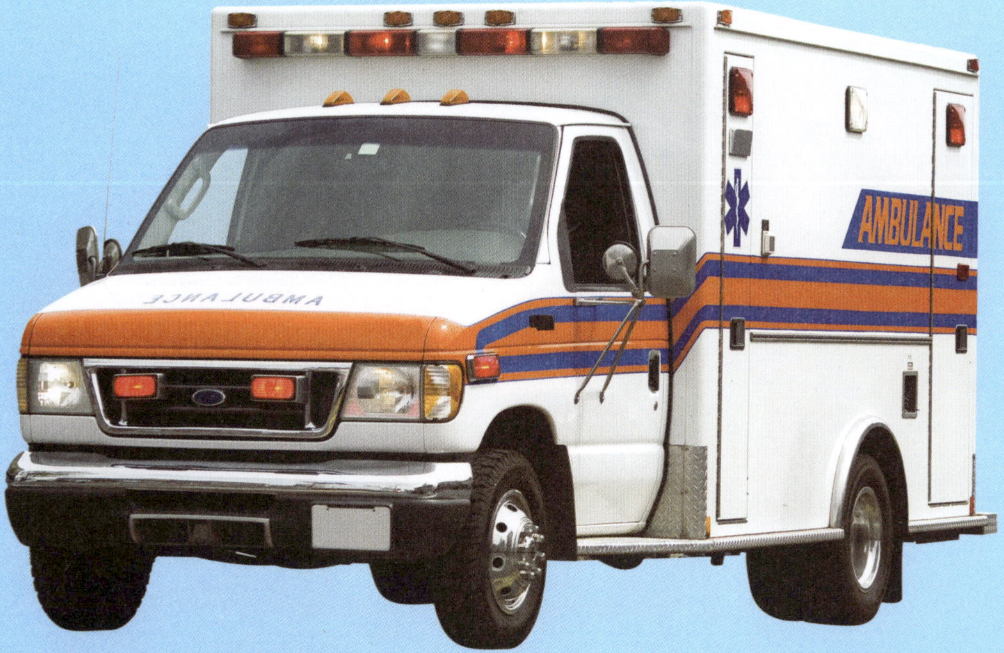

Ambulance

Tick (✓) the correct answer

Fire Engines are used by firefighters / doctors.

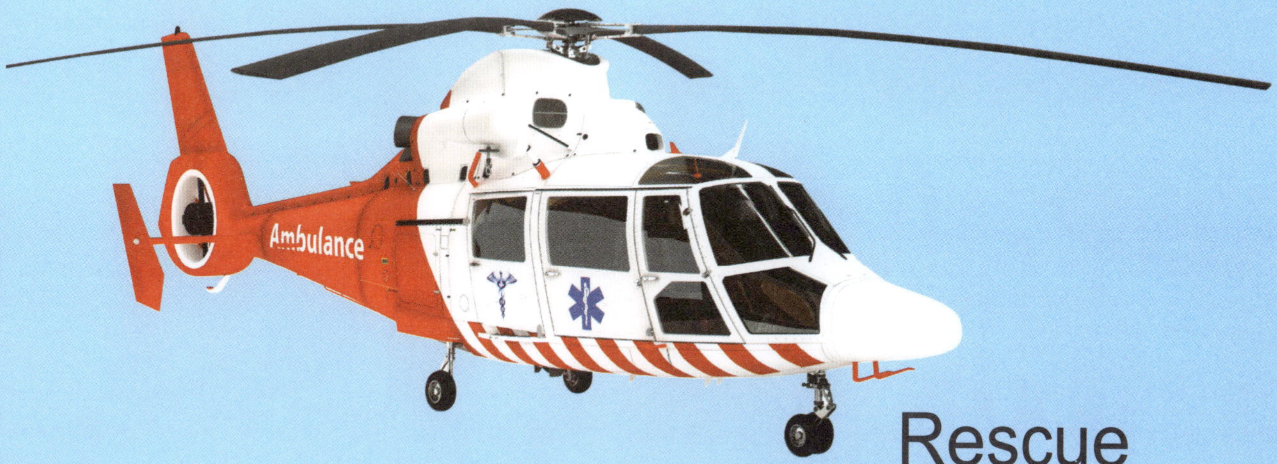

Rescue Helicopter

Rescue Boat

Tick (✓) the correct answer

Rescue Helicopters have wings / ears.

Car Carrier

Tanker

Tick (✓) the correct answer

Car Carriers transport people / cars.

Crane

Trailer Truck

Tick (✓) the correct answer

Cranes lift garbage / ocean.

Jet Plane

Tank

Tick (✓) the correct answer

Tanks are used by soldiers / teachers.

Torpedo
Boat

Drone

Tick (✓) the correct answer

Drones are used by military / writers.

Tractor

Digger

Tick (✓) the correct answer

Tractors are used by farmers / singers.

Forklift Truck

Harvester

Tick (✓) the correct answer

A Forklift Truck is a utensil / machine.

Gondola

Sledge

Tick (✓) the correct answer

A Sledge runs on snow / air.

Houseboat

Cocotaxi

Tick (✓) the correct answer

Houseboats are made of wood / water.

Robotic Car

Hybrid
Electric Bus

Tick (✓) the correct answer

Robotic Cars are automatic / magical.

Tick (✓) the correct answer

Electric Cars run on electricity / water.

Match the following

Helicopter • • 

Sailboat • • 

Airplane • • 

Bicycle • • 

Motorcycle • • 

Match the following

Tank ● ● 

Train ● ● 

Ferry Boat ● ● 

Jet Plane ● ● 

Car ● ● 

Cow

A cow gives milk / juice.

Calf

A calf eats fish / grass.

Sheep

A sheep gives us fruits / wool.

Lamb

A lamb is the baby of a sheep / parrot.

Cat

Tick (✓) the correct answer

A cat meows / quacks.

Kitten

A kitten is the young one of a cat / rat.

Goat

The baby of a goat is called kid / lamb.

Kid

Kids like to eat stones / grass.

Dog

Tick (✓) the correct answer

A dog lives in a kennel / tree.

Pup

A dog's baby is called a pencil / pup.

Horse

A horse lives in a building / stable.

Pony

A pony is the baby of a horse / ant.

Camel

A camel has a hump / trunk.

Camel Calf

A camel calf lives in a desert / ocean.

Hen

A hen lays eggs / burgers.

Chick

A hen's baby is a turkey / chick.

Turkey

The turkey is a big / small bird.

Poult

A turkey's baby is a poult / butterfly.

Rabbit

A rabbit has short / long ears.

Bunny

A bunny loves to eat carrots / pens.

Goose

A goose is reared in hospitals / farms.

Gosling

The baby of a goose is a gosling / candy.

Donkey

A donkey is a huge / tiny animal.

Foal

A donkey's baby is called a foal / snail.

Duck

A duck quacks / woofs.

Duckling

A duckling loves to swim in milk / water.

Alpaca

An alpaca is bred in farms / forests.

Cria

The baby of an alpaca is a cria / book.

Match the following

Kid • 

Pup • 

Calf • 

Cat • 

Hen • 

Match the following

Donkey

Poult

Duck

Horse

Cria

Cat

Fill in the blank

A c _ t is a furry ball of fun.

Kitten

Fill in the blank

A young cat is called k _ tten.

Horse

Fill in the blank

A ho _ se runs very fast.

Foal

Fill in the blank

A young horse is called a fo _ l.

Chimpanzee

Fill in the blank

A chim _ anzee can climb trees.

Infant

Fill in the blank

A young chimpanzee is called an infa _ t.

Deer

Fill in the blank

A d _ er eats grass.

Fawn

Fill in the blank

A young deer is called a fa _ n.

Elephant

Fill in the blank

An elephan _ has a trunk.

Calf

Fill in the blank

A young elephant is called a cal _ .

Lion

Fill in the blank

A li _ n is the ‘king of the jungle’.

Cub

Fill in the blank

A young lion is called a cu _ .

Giraffe

Fill in the blank

A gira _ fe has a long neck.

Calf

Fill in the blank

A young giraffe is called a c _ lf.

Tiger

Fill in the blank

A t _ ger can roar.

Cub

Fill in the blank

A young tiger is called a c _ b.

Match the following

Elephant • • 

Deer • • 

Cat • • 

Tiger • • 

Lion • •